HARRY'S MAGIC TABLES

Gill & Macmillan

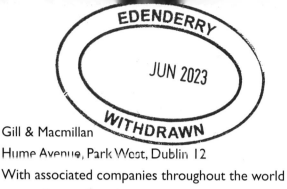

Gill & Macmillan
Hume Avenue, Park West, Dublin 12
With associated companies throughout the world
www.gillmacmillan.ie

© Stephanie Moraghan 2012

ISBN: 9780717151066

Print origination by Design Image, Dublin
Printed by Edelvives, Spain

The paper used in this book is made from the wood pulp of
managed forests. For every tree felled, at least one tree is planted,
thereby renewing natural resources.

Contents

Introduction   2

Harry's Top Tips for Children   3

Author's Tips for Teachers   4

Flying Rhymes   5

Running Rhymes   13

Jumping Rhymes   21

Painting Rhymes   27

Joker Rhymes   33

Wriggle Rhymes   37

Swinging Rhymes   41

Times Tables & Revision   43

Fun Quizzes   55

Note from the Author   62

Hi, my name is Harry and I'm nine years old. I'm in 3rd Class at school. This past year we started to learn our multiplication tables.

I did all my homework and tried very hard but I kept mixing up or forgetting my tables. I hated them!

But then Mum came to my rescue and made me this book!

After seven days, I knew as far as my 10 times tables. I also learnt 28 rhymes (four a day) and knew 110 tables off by heart. Magic!

It was easy to learn! I practised a lot by writing them out on paper first. Then Mum would ask me the rhymes on the way to and from school.

A few weeks later, my teacher gave me two pages of mental maths multiplication and division questions for homework. This would have normally taken me half an hour to finish but I had them done in five minutes. I also got every one of them right! I found division easy too because I knew my rhymes. Best of all, it was fun...fun...fun!

Follow my tips and you will do great too!

Harry's Top Tips For Children

1. Learn your rhymes in their groups, **Flying**, **Running Jumping** etc.

2. Learn the rhymes off by heart, as the answer always rhymes with the last word in the sentence.

3. Use the '*Flip it*' rule, as most of the rhymes apply to two different tables! For example:
   - The rhyme 'Three 9s **fly** off to **heaven**, 3 x 9 = **27**', is the same rhyme used for 9 x 3, just *flip it* and it becomes 3 x 9. Then repeat the rhyme 'Three 9s **fly** off to **heaven**', 3 x 9 = **27**'.
   - The rhyme 'Four 8s **run** after **you**, 4 x 8 = **32**' is the same rhyme used for 8 x 4, just *flip it* and it becomes 4 x 8. Then repeat the rhyme 'Four 8s **run** after **you**, 4 x 8 = **32**'.

4. Remember the lower number picks the type of rhyme you need. If you have 4 x 4, it's a **running** rhyme but if you have 4 x 3, it's a **flying rhyme!**

5. Chat about the pictures with your parents and friends, as it will help you to remember the rhymes.

6. Practise mental maths questions on paper first and you will get much quicker at remembering the answers.

7. There are no rhymes for 1, 2 or 10 times tables. They are too easy to need rhymes.

8. My most important tip is to never give up! Learning multiplication tables this way is FUN…FUN…FUN!

Author's Tips for Teachers – at school and at home!

1. Teach this book according to their groups, for example: **Flying** rhymes apply when **3** is the lower number; **Running** rhymes apply when **4** is the lower number etc.

2. Take time to explain the method...the lower number determines the type of rhyme it is.

    Example A:
    9 x **7**, **7** x 9 and 8 x **7** are all **joker** rhymes because **7** is the lower number.

    Example B:
    6 x **5**, 9 x **5** and **5** x 7 are all **jumping** rhymes because **5** is the lower number.

3. Spend time teaching each group of rhymes. When the children apply it on paper, it's amazing how fast they get it.

4. Discuss and enjoy the funny characters in the pictures, as this is also an important part of the learning process.

5. Don't over think the book! It is designed for those that don't already know their tables.

6. If you divide 28 rhymes by four weeks, it means learning seven rhymes per week. If that's not manageable, try one rhyme a day over the course of a month.

7. After lots of practice, the children will no longer need to rely on the full rhymes, as they will have their tables memorized to a fine art. This is how Harry now gets his answers and very quickly too!

    3 x 8 and 8 x 3...he thinks (**fly**, **door**) = **24**
    3 x 9 and 9 x 3...he thinks (**fly**, **heaven**) = **27**
    4 x 7 and 7 x 4...he thinks (**run**, **late**) = **28**
    4 x 6 and 6 x 4...he thinks (**run**, **door**) = **24**

8. Give it a chance!

Flying Rhymes

When 3 is the lower number in the table

Three 3s **fly** in ready to **dine**

$$3 \times 3 = 9$$

Three 4s **fly** in dressed as **elves**

We make twelve!

3 x 4 = 12

When teacher asks, 'What is 4 x 3?' flip the numbers over to 3 x 4 and remember this rhyme for the correct answer.

Three 5s **fly** shouting five-ten-fifteen

$$3 \times 5 = 15$$

When teacher asks, 'What is '5 x 3?' flip the numbers over to 3 x 5 and remember this rhyme for the correct answer.

Three 6s **fly** with wings bright **green**

3 x 6 = 18

When teacher asks 'What is 6 x 3?' flip the numbers over to 3 x 6 and remember this rhyme for the correct answer.

Three 7s **fly** into the **sun**

3 x 7 = 21

When teacher asks 'What is 7 x 3?' flip the numbers over to 3 x 7 and remember this rhyme for the correct answer.

Three 8s fly behind the door

24

3 x 8 = 24

11

When teacher asks 'What is 8 x 3?' flip the numbers over to 3 x 8 and remember this rhyme for the correct answer.

Three 9s fly off to heaven

3 x 9 = 27

When teacher asks 'What is 9 x 3?' flip the numbers over to 3 x 9 and remember this rhyme for the correct answer.

Running Rhymes

When 4 is the lower number in the table

Four 4s **run** after Bus **16**

$$4 \times 4 = 16$$

Four 5s **run** for fruit – there's **plenty**!

apples 20c

bananas 20c

$4 \times 5 = 20$

15

When teacher asks 'What is 5 x 4?' flip the numbers over to 4 x 5 and remember this rhyme for the correct answer.

Four 6s **run** to the **door**

$$4 \times 6 = 24$$

When teacher asks 'What is 6 x 4?' flip the numbers over to 4 x 6 and remember this rhyme for the correct answer.

Four 7s **run** when they are **late**

$$4 \times 7 = 28$$

When teacher asks 'What is 7 x 4?' flip the numbers over to 4 x 7 and remember this rhyme for the correct answer.

Four 8s **run** after **you**

$$4 \times 8 = 32$$

When teacher asks 'What is 8 x 4?' flip the numbers over to 4 x 8 and remember this rhyme for the correct answer.

Four 9s **run** taking **kicks**

4 x 9 = 36

When teacher asks 'What is 9x 4?' flip the numbers over to 4 x 9 and remember this rhyme for the correct answer.

Quiz

Flying and Running Rhymes

Before moving on, let's check how well you know your seven **Flying** rhymes and your six **Running** rhymes!

Think of the rhymes and the pictures. Now try to remember the two important words!

3 x 3	fly	dine	=	9
3 x 4			=	
3 x 5			=	
3 x 6	fly	green	=	18
3 x 7			=	
3 x 8			=	
3 x 9			=	
4 x 4	run	16	=	16
4 x 5			=	
4 x 6	run	door	=	24
4 x 7			=	
4 x 8			=	
4 x 9			=	

Jumping Rhymes

When 5 is the lower number in the table

Five 5s jump from the high dive

5 x 5 = 25

Five 6s jump in mud so dirty

5 x 6 = 30

23

When teacher asks 'What is 6 x 5?' flip the numbers over to 5 x 6 and remember this rhyme for the correct answer.

Five 7s jump
and bump a hive

5 x 7 = 35

24

When teacher asks 'What is 7 x 5?' flip the numbers over to 5 x 7 and remember this rhyme for the correct answer.

Five 8s jump and behave really naughty

5 x 8 = 40

25

When teacher asks, 'What is 8 x 5?' flip the numbers over to 5 x 8 and remember this rhyme for the correct answer.

Five 9s **jump** into cars and **drive**

5 x 9 = 45

When teacher asks, 'What is 9 x 5?' flip the numbers over to 5 x 9 and remember this rhyme for the correct answer.

Painting Rhymes

When 6 is the lower number in the table

Six 6s paint the bricks for kicks

$$6 \times 6 = 36$$

Six 7s **paint** with sticky **glue**

6 x 7 = 42

When teacher asks 'What is 7 x 6?' flip the numbers over to 6 x 7 and remember this rhyme for the correct answer.

Six 8s paint the garden gate

6 x 8 = 48

When teacher asks, 'What is 8 x 6?' flip the numbers over to 6 x 8 and remember this rhyme for the correct answer.

Six 9s **paint** numbers, it's a **chore**

$$6 \times 9 = 54$$

When teacher asks 'What is 9 x 6?' flip the numbers over to 6 x 9 and remember this rhyme for the correct answer.

Quiz

Jumping and Painting Rhymes

Before moving on, let's check how well you know your five **Jumping** rhymes and your four **Painting** rhymes!

Think of the rhymes and the pictures. Now try to remember the two important words!

5 x 5	jump	dive	=	25
5 x 6			=	
5 x 7	jump	hive	=	35
5 x 8			=	
5 x 9			=	
6 x 6	paint	kicks	=	36
6 x 7			=	
6 x 8			=	
6 x 9			=	

Joker Rhymes

When 7 is the lower number in the table

Seven **joker** 7s check the **time**

7 x 7 = 49

Seven **joker** 8s playing **tricks**

7 x 8 = 56

When teacher asks 'What is 8 x 7?' flip the numbers over to 7 x 8 and remember this rhyme for the correct answer.

Seven **joker** 9s sitting in a **tree**

7 x 9 = 63

36

Wriggle Rhymes

When 8 is the lower number in the table

Eight 8s **wriggle** on the **floor**

$$8 \times 8 = 64$$

Eight 9s wriggle on a shoe

€72

8 x 9 = 72

When teacher asks 'What is 9 x 8?' flip the numbers over to 8 x 9 and remember this rhyme for the correct answer.

Joker and Wriggle Rhymes

Before moving on, let's check how well you know your three **Joker** rhymes and your two **Wriggle** rhymes!

Think of the rhymes and the pictures. Now try to remember the two important words!

7 x 7	joker	time	=	49
7 x 8	joker	tricks	=	56
7 x 9			=	
8 x 8	wriggle	floor	=	64
8 x 9			=	

Swinging Rhymes

When 9 is the lower number in the table

Nine 9s **swinging** and having **fun**

9 x 9 = 81

Times
Tables

$$1 \times 0 = 0$$
$$1 \times 1 = 1$$
$$1 \times 2 = 2$$
$$1 \times 3 = 3$$
$$1 \times 4 = 4$$
$$1 \times 5 = 5$$
$$1 \times 6 = 6$$
$$1 \times 7 = 7$$
$$1 \times 8 = 8$$
$$1 \times 9 = 9$$
$$1 \times 10 = 10$$

$$2 \times 0 = 0$$
$$2 \times 1 = 2$$
$$2 \times 2 = 4$$
$$2 \times 3 = 6$$
$$2 \times 4 = 8$$
$$2 \times 5 = 10$$
$$2 \times 6 = 12$$
$$2 \times 7 = 14$$
$$2 \times 8 = 16$$
$$2 \times 9 = 18$$
$$2 \times 10 = 20$$

$$3 \times 0 = 0$$
$$3 \times 1 = 3$$
$$3 \times 2 = 6$$
$$3 \times 3 = 9$$
$$3 \times 4 = 12$$
$$3 \times 5 = 15$$
$$3 \times 6 = 18$$
$$3 \times 7 = 21$$
$$3 \times 8 = 24$$
$$3 \times 9 = 27$$
$$3 \times 10 = 30$$

4	x	0	=	0
4	x	1	=	4
4	x	2	=	8
4	x	3	=	12
4	x	4	=	16
4	x	5	=	20
4	x	6	=	24
4	x	7	=	28
4	x	8	=	32
4	x	9	=	36
4	x	10	=	40

$$5 \times 0 = 0$$
$$5 \times 1 = 5$$
$$5 \times 2 = 10$$
$$5 \times 3 = 15$$
$$5 \times 4 = 20$$
$$5 \times 5 = 25$$
$$5 \times 6 = 30$$
$$5 \times 7 = 35$$
$$5 \times 8 = 40$$
$$5 \times 9 = 45$$
$$5 \times 10 = 50$$

6	x	0	=	0
6	x	1	=	6
6	x	2	=	12
6	x	3	=	18
6	x	4	=	24
6	x	5	=	30
6	x	6	=	36
6	x	7	=	42
6	x	8	=	48
6	x	9	=	54
6	x	10	=	60

7	x	0	=	0
7	x	1	=	7
7	x	2	=	14
7	x	3	=	21
7	x	4	=	28
7	x	5	=	35
7	x	6	=	42
7	x	7	=	49
7	x	8	=	56
7	x	9	=	63
7	x	10	=	70

$8 \times 0 = 0$

$8 \times 1 = 8$

$8 \times 2 = 16$

$8 \times 3 = 24$

$8 \times 4 = 32$

$8 \times 5 = 40$

$8 \times 6 = 48$

$8 \times 7 = 56$

$8 \times 8 = 64$

$8 \times 9 = 72$

$8 \times 10 = 80$

$$9 \times 0 = 0$$
$$9 \times 1 = 9$$
$$9 \times 2 = 18$$
$$9 \times 3 = 27$$
$$9 \times 4 = 36$$
$$9 \times 5 = 45$$
$$9 \times 6 = 54$$
$$9 \times 7 = 63$$
$$9 \times 8 = 72$$
$$9 \times 9 = 81$$
$$9 \times 10 = 90$$

10	x	0	=	0
10	x	1	=	10
10	x	2	=	20
10	x	3	=	30
10	x	4	=	40
10	x	5	=	50
10	x	6	=	60
10	x	7	=	70
10	x	8	=	80
10	x	9	=	90
10	x	10	=	100

Revision

Remember, the lower number in the table decides what rhyme you need!

When **3** is the lower number in the table, it is always a **flying** rhyme.

When **4** is the lower number in the table, it is always a **running** rhyme.

When **5** is the lower number in the table, it is always a **jumping** rhyme.

When **6** is the lower number in the table, it is always a **painting** rhyme.

When **7** is the lower number in the table, it is always a **joker** rhyme.

When **8** is the lower number in the table, it is always a **wriggle** rhyme.

When **9** is the lower number in the table, it is always a **swinging** rhyme.

Fun Quizzes

Quiz 1

Example 1:

Q. 4 x 7 = which rhyme?

A. The **running** rhyme, because **4** is the lower number.
Four 7s **run** when they are **late**
4 x 7 = **28**

Example 2:

Q. 8 x 3 = which rhyme?

A. The **flying** rhyme, because **3** is the lower number.
So use the *Flip it rule* to remember the 3 x 8 rhyme.
Three 8s **fly** behind the **door**
3 x 8 = 24

It's Your Turn!

3 x 5 = which rhyme?

6 x 3 = which rhyme?

9 x 4 = which rhyme?

7 x 8 = which rhyme?

8 x 6 = which rhyme?

5 x 9 = which rhyme?

4 x 4 = which rhyme?

*2 x 3 = has no rhyme as the table
has a lower number than 3

Quiz 2

Let's practise the *flip it* rule!

Example: 4 x 3 = ?
Flip it over to **3** x **4** and it becomes a **flying** rhyme.
Three 4s **fly** in dressed as **elves**
3 x 4 = 12

Now you try:

- 8 x **7** = (flip it to) _____ and it becomes

  a _____ rhyme.

  Write the rhyme: _____

- 9 x **4** = (flip it to) _____ and it becomes

  a _____ rhyme.

  Write the rhyme: _____

- 8 x **6** = (flip it to) _____ and it becomes

  a _____ rhyme.

  Write the rhyme: _____

- 9 x **3** = (flip it to) _____ and it becomes

  a _____ rhyme.

  Write the rhyme: _____

- 7 x **5** = (flip it to) _____ and it becomes

  a _____ rhyme.

  Write the rhyme: _____

Quiz 3

Picture Quiz

Let's see what you can remember from the pictures in the rhymes.

1. 3 x 3 (**flying** 3s) – how much does the menu cost?

2. 3 x 4 (**flying** 4s) – what are they dressed as?

3. 3 x 5 (**flying** 5s) – what are they shouting?

4. 3 x 6 (**flying** 6s) – what colour are their wings?

5. 3 x 7 (**flying** 7s) – how hot is the sunny day?

6. 3 x 8 (**flying** 8s) – what number is on the door?

7. 3 x 9 (**flying** 9s) – what is the name of the airline?

8. 4 x 4 (**running** 4s) – what number is on the bus?

9. 4 x 5 (**running** 5s) – what price are the apples and bananas?

10. 4 x 6 (**running** 6s) – what number is on the door?

11. 4 x 7 (**running** 7s) – how late are they?

12. 4 x 8 (**running** 8s) – what number is on their shoes?

13. 4 x 9 (**running** 9s) – what's the score on the scoreboard?

14. 5 x 5 (**jumping** 5s) – how high is the high dive?

15. 5 x 6 (jumping 6s) – what temperature is on the box of washing powder?

16. 5 x 7 (jumping 7s) – how many bees are in the hive?

17. 5 x 8 (jumping 8s) – what number is on the balloons?

18. 5 x 9 (jumping 9s) – what number is on the racing car?

19. 6 x 6 (painting 6s) – what number do the bricks make?

20. 6 x 7 (painting 7s) – what number is the sticky glue squirting out?

21. 6 x 8 (painting 8s) – what number is on the gate?

22. 6 x 9 (painting 9s) – what number are they painting?

23. 7 x 7 (joker 7s) – how many minutes are on their watches?

24. 7 x 8 (joker 8s) – what number is on the card of spades?

25. 7 x 9 (joker 9s) – what number do the falling leaves make?

26. 8 x 8 (wriggle 8s) – how many bugs did the fat snake eat?

27. 8 x 9 (wriggle 9s) – how much does the shoe cost?

28. 9 x 9 (swinging 9s) – what number are they swinging on?

Quiz 4

Rhyme Quiz

Let's see how well you remember your rhymes!
Fill in the blanks below.

1. Nine 9s _____ and having _____, $9 \times 9 =$ _____

2. Seven _____ 8s playing _____, $7 \times 8 =$ _____

3. Six 8s _____ the garden _____, $6 \times 8 =$ _____

4. _____ 9s run _____ kicks, $4 \times 9 =$ _____

5. Three _____ fly off to _____, $3 \times$ _____ $= 27$

6. Five 9s _____ into _____ and _____,
   $5 \times 9 =$ _____

7. Eight 8s _____ on the _____, $8 \times 8 =$ _____

8. _____ 9s wriggle on ___ _____, $8 \times 9 =$ _____

9. Seven Joker 7s _____ ___ _____, $7 \times 7 =$ _____

10. Six _____ paint _____ sticky _____,
    $6 \times 7 =$ _____

11. Three 7s _____ into the _____, $3 \times 7 =$ _____

12. Four _____ run after _____, $4 \times 8 =$ _____

13. Six 9s _____ numbers, it's a _____, $6 \times 9 =$
    _____

14. Three 6s fly with _____ _____ _____,
    $3 \times 6 =$ _____

15. Five 8s _____ and behave really _____,
    5 x 8 = _____

16. Four 7s run when they _____ _____,
    4 x 7 = _____

17. Seven _____ 9s sitting ___ ___ _____,
    7 x 9 = _____

18. Three 3s fly in ready to _____, 3 x 3 = _____

19. Three _____ fly in dressed _____ _____,
    3 x _____ = 12

20. Six 6s _____ the bricks for _____, 6 x 6 = 36

21. Five 5s jump _____ the _____ _____,
    5 x 5 = _____

22. Four 5s _____ for _____ – there's _____!
    4 x 5 = _____

23. Five 6s _____ in _____ so _____, 5 x 6 = 30

24. Four 4s _____ after _____ _____,
    4 x 4 = _____

25. Three 5s fly _____ five– ten– _____,
    3 x 5 = _____

26. Four 6s _____ to the _____, 4 x 6 = _____

27. Three _____ fly behind _____ _____,
    3 x = _____

28. Five 7s _____ and _____ a _____, 5 x 7 = 35

Note from the Author

To all teachers, parents and children, I hope you found this method of learning multiplication tables as much fun as Harry did. He is simply bursting with confidence and really enjoys doing his maths homework now.

I would like to thank Harry, Sonya, Sheila, Catherine, Pamela, Ciaran and Ms. Hickey for their encouragement. I'd also like to thank the editorial team at Gill & Macmillan for making this book possible. Harry would especially like to thank Jonathan.